To request permission, contact the author
at author@sunburstcitydragons.co.uk

ISBN number: 978-1-8383080-4-9

Second edition June 2021
Author: Jane Huddleston
Illustrations and formatting: David Robinson

www.sunburstcitydragons.co.uk

THEO'S BIRTHDAY

Written by
Jane Huddleston

Illustrated by
David Robinson

Outside Sunburst City, where the hills are wild and green,
Live a group of ten old dragons that most humans haven't seen.
They work and have adventures in a secret world of wonder,
While living in a hidden cave that's halfway up Mount Thunder.
They sneak around so humans don't know where they all have been,
Just two brave children help their dragon friends remain unseen.

Theo's a mechanic
Bob announces for the trains
Lucy is an athelete
Harry unblocks drains
Millie is a writer
Olive farms the land
Alice is a scientist
Jack makes chairs by hand
Yellowbeard's a pirate, now retired with creaking knees
Isla is a bee keeper, she's busy keeping bees.

HARRY

MILLIE

OLIVE

JACK

YELLOWBEARD

ISLA

Theo is the biggest one at seventeen foot tall.
He's purple with green patches and just loves to kick a ball.
An excellent mechanic fixing anything on wheels,
While he's hidden in a garage pit to work and eat his meals.
Theo loves his football, so he trains with all his might,
But so that humans didn't see he always trains at night.

This day was Theo's birthday, he was happy as could be.
Excited he was now a chipper one hundred and three.
His dragon friends were planning on his birthday at nightfall,
They would throw a birthday party with a cake shaped like a ball.
This present would be perfect, he would think it was so sweet,
To combine his favourite team game with his favourite thing to eat.

These dragon friends are never seen but certainly are heard,
Being expert on the telephone and at the written word.
On the far side of Mount Thunder a communication mast,
Means their internet connection's always super-duper fast.

Bob searched the internet and phoned a baker in the town,
Who would bake a giant cake but as he wrote the order down,
He questioned 'Three foot wide, Sir? Are you sure that size is right?
Will the people at your party have a super appetite?!'

Bob laughed a flame filled giggle as he reassured the baker,
'Yes a three foot football please! Will it be ready later?''
It will' the baker promised, 'you can pick it up at four,
But I'm really quite concerned about it fitting through the door.'

At times like this the dragons really need a chaperone,
For an order can't be picked up by a dragon on his own.
The Sunburst City dragons had two friends who were so helpful,
And in keeping dragons secret they had proven fundamental.
Matt and Alex Walker lived nearby and could be trusted,
They would often help hide dragon clues so none of them got busted.

Bob let out his special roar and patiently did wait,
For the children to come running to their hidden garden gate.
He told them of his brilliant plan to get the cake at four,
But he'd need their help to get it as he cannot use the door.
The children told their parents they would play out for a while,
Then they jumped upon the dragons back and flew off with a smile.

They landed near the back door of the bakers in the street,
Knowing Bob had made a cunning plan of how to move the treat.
The children paid the baker saying 'Thanks, the cake is great!',
While Bob lifted up the kitchen roof, tied ropes around the plate.
He raised the cake up slowly, staying out of humans' sight,
Then the children ran back laughing and got ready for the flight.

The dragon flapped his wings and they took off to fly up high,
Thinking 'This must be the only birthday treat up in the sky!'
As they placed the football cake upon the pitch that's on Mount Thunder,
They smiled with joy that all went well, without a single blunder!

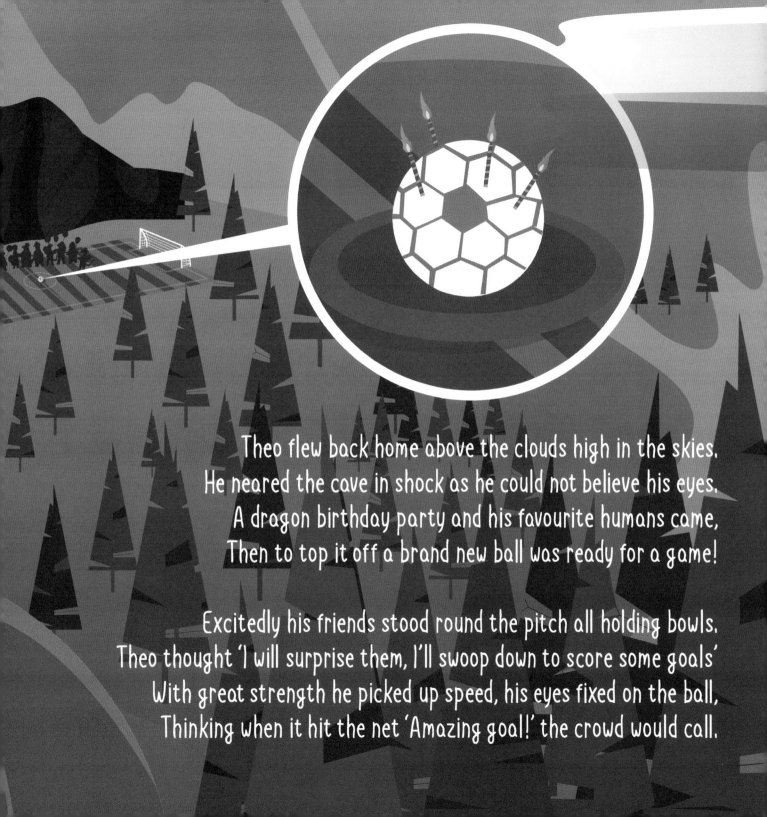

Theo flew back home above the clouds high in the skies.
He neared the cave in shock as he could not believe his eyes.
A dragon birthday party and his favourite humans came,
Then to top it off a brand new ball was ready for a game!

Excitedly his friends stood round the pitch all holding bowls.
Theo thought 'I will surprise them, I'll swoop down to score some goals'
With great strength he picked up speed, his eyes fixed on the ball,
Thinking when it hit the net 'Amazing goal!' the crowd would call.

He flew down low with wings out wide to where the ball was sat,
Then pulled back his claw and swung his leg to give the ball a whack!
But as his front claw struck the ball his friends all gasped in fright.
Theo thought this ball was far too soft so something wasn't right.

Bits of cake flew through the air and splatted in the bowls,
The penny dropped as Theo laughed, 'I didn't score some goals,
But better still the cake is served!' they burst into applause,
While the birthday dragon ate his treat straight off his sticky claws.

Bob flew the children home while all the others tidied up.
Theo loved his birthday party and could not believe his luck.
Dragon clans around the world heard of this party, no mistake,
As the only birthday party where a dragon kicked the cake!

Next time you're at the baker's and you see the cakes to eat,
Just think maybe that baker baked a dragon's birthday treat.
Look all around, check high and low, for clues you may have missed,
For if you find a few you may prove dragons do exist!

Printed in Great Britain
by Amazon